Ladybird would like to thank Jane Swift for additional illustration work.

Published by Ladybird Books Ltd
A Penguin Company
Penguin Books Ltd, 80 Strand, London WC2R 0RL, UK
Penguin Books Australia Ltd, Camberwell, Victoria, Australia
Penguin Books (NZ) Ltd, Cnr Airbourne and Rosedale Roads, Albany, Auckland, 1310, New Zealand
3 5 7 9 10 8 6 4 2

Printed in Italy

Busy Shop

written by Melanie Joyce
illustrated by Sue King

Ladybird

It's a busy day at Busy Shop.

Ting-a-ling, rings the Busy Shop be

Here's another customer for Lotty and Dot.

"Good morning, Molly," they say.

Molly's here to buy groceries.
The twins have come along, too.

"Mummy has shopping to do,"
she says to them.
"Behave yourselves!"
Do you think they will?

Polly and Max play hide and seek.
They run up and down the aisles.

Max finds Polly's hiding place.
He jumps out and shouts, "BOO!"
But it isn't Polly he has found.
Who do you think it is?

Poor Mrs Snipe gets such a fright.
She drops her shopping basket.
Everything falls all over the floor.

Luckily nothing is damaged.

"Sorry," says Max.

"Sorry," says Polly.

"We were only playing hide and seek."

"Don't worry," says Dot.
"We'll soon tidy up.
There's no harm done.
It was just some fun."

Mrs Snipe gives a sniff.

She struts off with her shopping.

"Come along," says Molly.

"It's time to go home."

And off they go.

Just then the bell *ting-a-lings*,
Stanley Stubbs comes
limping in.

He has fallen off his skateboard,
and has grazed his knee.
Poor Stanley, that looks sore.

"Don't worry," smiles Lotty. "We've got just the thing. Here's a plaster to put on your knee."

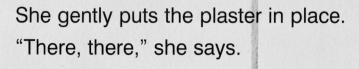

She gently puts the plaster in place.
"There, there," she says.

Not long after, the bell *ting-a-lings*.
The door flies wide open.

Mrs Skipps comes racing in.
She's nearly out of breath.
What do you think she says?

"Oh, dear, I tripped. I slipped. Jilly's party cake fell splat on the mat. It's totally squashed."

"Don't worry," smiles Dot.
"We've got just the thing."
And she brings out a large
white box.
But what's in it?

Inside the box is a beautiful cake.
It has pink sugar icing and
sugar flowers on top.

Mrs Skipps thinks it's wonderful!
Do you think Jilly likes it too?

Of course she does!
It's the best party cake ever.

"Thanks, Lotty and Dot," says
Mrs Skipps.
"You've really saved the day."

It has been a busy day at Busy Shop.
Now the bell is quiet.
The till is locked.

"Let's have a sit down," says Lotty
to Dot.
"It's our turn to have a treat."
And they've got just the thing!